JACK THE STAT GOES TO SCHOOL

Alan Cliff
Illustrated by Helen Maffin

**50% author royalties to
Winnicott Foundation
St Mary's Hospital, Paddington, London**

WWB CHILDREN'S
NORWICH, NR8 6YN

ISBN: 1-903264-20-0
Published by: Wendy Webb Books
Printed by: Catton Print, Norwich
Trade enquiries: 0798-917 4076
By post: Wendy Webb, PO Box 210, Taverham, NORWICH, NR8 6WX

British Library Cataloguing-in-Publication Data
A catalogue record for this book is available from the British Library.

Trademark Notice:
Jack The Station Cat is registered for trademark purposes. Merchandise
enquiries, in the first instance, should be made through Wendy Webb
Books.

WWB CHILDREN'S
Reading guide: 5-8 year olds.

ANSWERS TO THE ACTIVITY PAGES
A. 1. Marmalade; 2. George; 3. Paw; 4. Sniff; 5. Jack; 6. Purr; 7. Chicken;
8. Claws; 9. Secret; 10. First; 11. Bowls; 12. Naughty.
Mews Junction.
B. Green (flag).
C. Jack learned how it is sometimes wise to be in disguise.
D. paws; nose; eyes; ears; mouth.

Dads and Mums follow Jack's station capers at Lock's
Sidings in British Railway Modelling magazine and his
many thoughts in Words, Cambrensis, Linkway, Gentle
Reader and Furry Fables.

THE WINNICOTT FOUNDATION

St Mary's Hospital, Praed Street, London, W2.
Foreword by Shaun Peare, editor of WORDS short story magazine.

The Winnicott Foundation is a registered charity originally formed by parents whose children owe their lives to the Winnicott Baby Unit. It has grown into an active organisation supporting the vital work carried out in the Winnicott Baby Unit at St. Mary's Hospital, Praed Street, London W2.

In the forefront of specialist care for premature babies The Winnicott Baby Unit treats over 300 premature and sick new-born babies, most of who would not survive without expert care. These babies are born not only at St. Mary's but are also transferred from other hospitals without the facilities to care for them.

Our own daughter Charlotte – herself a Winnicott baby and now nearly seven years old – insists that the author Alan Cliff is indeed a friend of Jack the station cat's and that Jack is probably the cleverest cat in the whole world. His exploits are eagerly read every quarter in the pages of several small press magazines.

A percentage of the royalties from the sales of this book is being generously donated to The Winnicott Foundation (Registered Charity Number: 292668) by the author to help to buy the expensive equipment needed to look after these fragile babies. This will help the babies cope with the daily life or death crises that come with premature birth. His generosity can let the vital work that has given life to so many sick babies not only continue but to be further improved. Additional help is always urgently needed for this to be achieved.

The quarterly magazine "WORDS" is one of the many ways you can help to support the work being undertaken in the special baby unit - so why not think of taking out a regular subscription. Full details of current subscription rates - either for yourself or as a thoughtful gift - and a FREE sample copy can be had by writing to: WORDS, PO Box 13574, London W9 3FX

Finally grateful thanks go to Jack the station cat, his friend Alan Cliff and to Wendy Webb Books from the Winnicott Baby Unit, Words Magazine and indeed from my wife and I personally as we shall always be thankful for the part the unit played in our daughter's survival.

Shaun Peare, Editor, Words Magazine, 2000

There were big cats, small cats,
fat cats, thin cats.

"Scritch, scratch, scrunge."

JACK THE STATION CAT GOES TO SCHOOL

Scritch, scratch, scrunge. "Stop it, Jack!" shouted Mr Parker the Station Master. Jack the Station Cat was sharpening his claws on the carpet in the Station Master's office.

He jumped on his friend Peter the
Porter's shoulder.

Jack looked guilty and hopped back into his basket marked 'STATION CAT'.

"The early morning train is coming in, Jack," called Mr Parker.

The little black and white cat trotted onto the platform. He jumped on his friend Peter the Porter's shoulder and purred at the passengers.

"Morning, Jack," many of them called back.

Jack went back into the Station Master's office. "Scritch, scratch, scrunge."

"You are a **naughty, naughty** cat, Jack," the Station Master said. "I shall send you for a day to Mews Junction School for Station Cats. They'll teach you

to be a **First Class** Station Cat."
Jack sat in the corner and huffed!
Mr Parker fastened a ticket to Jack's collar. It read:
Tails End to Mews Junction Special Return.
"George the Guard will look after you," said Mr Parker.
Jack jumped into George's van.
George blew his whistle, waved his green flag and shouted "Right away."
Off went the train.

When they got to Mews Junction Jack was met by a small black cat called Stumpy.
"This way to the Station Cats' School," he said.

At the school were lots of other Station Cats. There were big cats, small cats, fat cats, thin cats, tabby cats, black cats, grey cats and white cats. They sat in a big circle on the floor. In the middle of the circle - on a piece of carpet - was a huge marmalade cat.

There were big cats, small cats, fat cats, thin cats.

"Now cats," growled Mr MacAllister.
"Lesson One: How to tell a box of fish."

"That's Mr MacAllister, our teacher," whispered Stumpy.

By Mr MacAllister were all sorts of boxes. "How interesting," thought Jack. "I wonder what's in them?"

"Hello, Jack," said Mr MacAllister. "Lessons are just about to start. Sit down there with Stumpy." He pointed to a gap in the circle.

"Now cats," growled Mr MacAllister. "Lesson One: **How to tell a box of fish.** Two boxes here. One has fish. One doesn't. How do you tell which is which? Sniff hard, cats. Sniff hard."

The cats gathered round the boxes. They sniffed and sniffed. Then they all pounced on one box.

"That's enough, cats," shouted Mr MacAllister. "Back to your places."

"Lesson Two: **Is the fish fresh? Just put your paw in - so.**" Mr MacAllister put his paw in the fish box and quickly pulled out a fish. "Slurp, slurp, munch!" Mr MacAllister ate the fish. "Never take more than **one** fish," he said sternly. "If your tummy's too full you can't check properly."
Jack was **very** interested in this lesson. Fish sometimes arrived at Tails End. "**Now** I know what to do with it," he thought.
"Lesson Three after break," said Mr MacAllister. "Bowls of milk behind the signal box."

When the cats went back to their classroom they had a surprise. Mr MacAllister wasn't there. In his placc was a big grey cat.

"It's all right, cats," this animal said. "I'm Mr MacAllister. I'm in disguise. That's what Lesson Three is about: **Disguises for Station Cats.** When testing fish you must do it in disguise.

"Slurp, slurp, munch!"

"Did you know your Great-Grandfather once tripped up a Prime Minister, Jack?"

It's a secret known only to cats," whispered Mr MacAllister. "Come closer and I'll tell you."

The cats all came close like a big furry ball. Their tails stuck out like bits of fuzzy string.

"Whisper... whisper... whisper," went Mr MacAllister.

"Lunch break now," said Mr MacAllister when the lesson was over. Mind you're back in time."

After a snack of tasty chicken all the cats were ready at 2.00. **"Do's and don'ts** is the first lesson this afternoon," said Mr MacAllister.

"Never get in a passenger's way. It's instant dismissal if you do. Did you know your Great-Grandfather once tripped up a Prime Minister, Jack? What's more, the Prime Minister lost his ticket when he fell."

"Oh dear," said Jack, and his whiskers drooped. "Did Great-Grandfather lose his job?"

"No, he didn't," replied Mr MacAllister. "He'd been testing fish and was in disguise. No-one knew who he was. Shows how important disguise is."

At that moment Jack's claws felt itchy. "I must scratch," he thought. "Ah! Mr MacAllister's carpet - perfect!"

He jumped out of the circle of cats onto the carpet on which Mr MacAllister sat. "Scritch, scratch, scrunge," he went.

"JACK!" roared Mr MacAllister. "STATION CATS **NEVER** SCRATCH THEIR CLAWS ON CARPETS."

Jack slunk back to his place. "I'm sorry," he said.

"I should think so," said MacAllister. "Always find a piece of wood or a tree in the yard."

"Now, cats," he said. Our last lesson. **Disappearing!**"
Suddenly Mr MacAllister vanished.

"Where is he?" shouted Jack. "Come on cats, let's find him. He can't be far."

"JACK!"
roared Mr
MacAllister.

**They searched everywhere: underneath
the boxes, inside the boxes.**

18

The cats searched the shed. No sign of Mr MacAllister. They looked everywhere: underneath the boxes, **inside** the boxes, behind some old planks in the corner.

"He must be hiding in that old sack by the door!" one of the cats shouted. But he wasn't.

"It's no use, cats," said Jack. "Mr MacAllister's not here."

"End of lesson, everyone," said a familiar voice.

Jack thought the sound came from the carpet. He looked hard at it. Sitting there, still as still, as though he were part of the pattern, was Mr MacAllister.

"There he is!" shouted Jack.

"That's the end of lessons," announced Mr MacAllister.

"Here's your train, Jack," shouted Stumpy.

George the Guard stepped out when the train stopped. "Come along, Jack," he called.

Jack leaped into the van and sat on a box. George stepped in. "Right away!" he called, and off they went.

Jack sniffed. "I can smell fish," he thought. "I think it's in the box I'm sitting on."

When George wasn't looking Jack slipped a paw in the box just like Mr MacAllister had. Out came a fish. "I'll just check to see it's fresh," Jack said to himself as he swallowed it.

"Tails End! Tails End!" shouted Peter the Porter. Jack was

home. He jumped out of the van and went straight to the Station Master's office.

"So you're back, Jack," said Mr Parker. "I hope you learned a lot."

Jack was just going to sharpen his claws on the carpet when he remembered about his Great-Grandfather. "I don't want to lose my job as Station Cat over a bit of carpet," he thought.

"Scritch, scratch, scrunge."

So he went out into the station yard, found a piece of wood and scratched his claws on that. "Scritch, scratch, scrunge."

Mr Parker was watching through his window. "I think Mews School has done Jack good," he said.

THE END

Now try the Activities on pages 23-24.

"I think
Mews
School has
done Jack
good."

ACTIVITY PAGES

Complete word puzzle using clues below.

A.

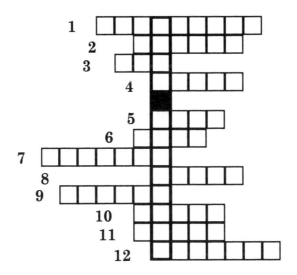

1. Mr MacAllister was this colour.
2. The name of the guard.
3. A cat's foot.
4. To tell which box contained fish, the cats had to do this.
5. A famous station cat.
6. The noise a happy cat makes.
7. The cats had this for dinner at Mews Junction School.
8. Cats should never sharpen these on carpets.
9. Mr MacAllister whispered one of these to the cats.
10. After being at school Jack would be this class of station cat.

ACTIVITY PAGES

11. Milk was served to the cats in these.
12. Jack was this before he went to school.
Now read down the grid for two more words:
What place made Jack feel he was still at school?

B. There are five colours mentioned in the story. Only one is not the colour of a cat. Which colour?

C. Can you read this message? It's written in code. The code is given below.
E.g: Qzxp = Jack.

Qzxp ovzimvw sld rg rh hlnvgrnvh drhv gl yv rm wrhtfrhv.

CODE: a=z b=y c=x d=w e=v f=u g=t h=s I=r j=q k=p l=o m=n n=m o=l p=k q=j r=I s=h t=g u=f v=e w=d x=c y=b z=a

D. Jack used all five senses (touch, smell, sight, hearing, taste). Complete the sentences:
With his _____ Jack touched Peter's shoulder.
With his _____ Jack smelt the fish.
With his _____ Jack saw Stumpy.
With his _____ Jack heard the whistle.
With his _____ Jack tasted the chicken.
Answers on page 2.